Wynter Sommers

I0647313

EDGES

Book 10

Conversation Station

Guide Book for the EDGES series

Bjorn Esterday Was Not Born Yesterday

Wynter Sommers

Wynter Sommers

USA Copyright © 2017 Susan E dePillis & GJ dePillis

TXu001885818
PAu 3-627-478, 1-798104171, PAu003401882, PAu003759141,
1-787-353831
Library of Congress Control Number: 2019930942

Published by Pure Force Enterprises, Inc.
California, USA
Since 2002

ISBN-13: 978-1-7184-0011-5
ISBN-10:1-7184-0011-X

DEDICATION

To all teachers, home-schoolers, community organizers, travelers, book clubs, students and people who want to have engaging, thoroughly exploratory, conversation. This book will hone critical thinking skills to promote lively conversation with other human beings. We hope your hearts reach out to change the world around you for the better. We know your minds will creatively decipher the next strategic move, making your world a nicer place for everyone. We souls crave adventure and value the freedoms of democracy. This set of questions and conversation starters are dedicated to nourish the spirit within you. We l earnestly wish you great success as you harness the power of fiction to bring new perspectives to reality as you make tomorrow a better place for everyone.

CONTENTS

How To Use This Book

This book is designed to guide activities for anywhere from one to a great many students. It can be used by classroom instructors, community planners, reading clubs, and homeschooling guides. The sections help to stimulate critical thinking by opening up topics of conversation and suggesting some activities.

There are no tests with answers in this lesson plan guide. The lack of tests was intentional as the learning approach is to be interactive and not rote memorization of facts which can be copied.

Suggested Reading Order for the EDGES Series

EDGES BOOK 1-SWIFT ENCOUNTER
EDGES BOOK 2-ROUSING ATTACK
EDGES BOOK 3-ONE FOOT UNDER
EDGES BOOK 4-EARTHSHAKE
EDGES BOOK 5-BROKEN STRING
EDGES BOOK 6-KEY WITNESS
EDGES BOOK 7-WHO IS SHE?
EDGES BOOK 8-VANISH
EDGES BOOK 9-CHASE OR DIE

Alternate Reading plan for books starring Bjorn & Sarah

1st   Edges Book 1
2nd   Edges Book 2
3rd   Gone Book 1
4th   Firebrand Book 1
5th   Edges Book 3
6th   Firebrand Book 2
7th   Gone Book 2
8th   Gone Book 3
9th   Firebrand Book 3
10th Gone Book 4
11th Firebrand Book 4
12th Gone Book 5
13th Gone Book 6
14th Edges Book 4
15th Firebrand Book 5
16th Gone Book 7
17th Firebrand Book 6
18th Gone Book 8
19th Firebrand Book 7
20th Gone Book 9
21st Firebrand Book 8
22nd Gone Book 10
23rd Gone Book 11
24th Gone Book 12
25th Gone Book 13
26th Firebrand Book 9 (End)
27th Gone Book 14
28th Gone Book 15
29th Gone Book 16
30th Gone Book 17
31st Gone Book 18 (End)
32nd Edges Book 5
33rd Edges Book 6
34th Edges Book 7
35th Edges Book 8
36th Edges Book 9 (End)

Main Characters

- **Sarah Paradise** - School Teacher
- **Bjorn Esterday** - Reporter at the Daily Memo Newspaper. Works for Sammy Scribe.
- **Percy Snatcher** - Head of the AnCor cell
- **Slash** - Loyal AnCor follower of Percy
- **Noah Lantz** - Earth Farmer husband to Ruth Lantz
- **Joshua Lantz** - Earth Farmer child of Ruth and Noah Lantz
- **Ruth Lantz** - Earth Farmer Mother to Joshua. Wife to Noah. Expert quilter.
- **Jack Courtly** - Head of Courtly City. Jack is Queenie's husband. Jack is athletic, disciplined, handsome and has a character based on integrity, which is demonstrated by his consideration for his family members. Jack's older brother is Skipper. Jack's child is Ace.
- **Queenie Courtly** -Wife to Jack Courtly
- **Ace Courtly** - Child of Jack and Queenie Courtly

- **Skipper Courtly** - . Skipper is the older brother to Jack, the current leader of Courtly City. Skipper, as the eldest, resents that he was passed up by Jack to run Courtly Dynamics Corporation. Skipper's passions include eating, status, fashion, and parties. He lacks determination but demands to be in charge. He only uses friendly gestures to manipulate others to get what he wants. He can be obsequious if he is challenged by a more powerful bully.
- **Pip Courtly** - Child of Skipper Courtly
- **Widow Medicina**- Courtly City citizen and train passenger, recently widowed.
- **Mrs Libris** - Librarian
- **Sammy Scribe**- Editor of Daily Memo Newspaper and Bjorn's boss.
- **Guard Gene**- Courtly City guard who also works at the Men's prison.

EDGES Book Subject Preparation

This section is dedicated to the purpose of challenging students who have started to read the book, to consider these fictional parallels with the real world. Exercises will hone the student's critical thinking skills. Such questions address concepts brought up by the book and are not assigned to any single chapter. For chapter-specific questions, please see the chapters headed with the relevant book title.

Let's Begin...

1. What role do libraries play in society today?

2. Should horses become mainstream modes of transportation today and replace vehicles which need fuel? Why or Why not?

3. Sarah teaches her classroom children how to turn pages properly. What other simple skills do you employ which might be lost due to technology replacing that action?

4. What is the point of the HIB in this story and do you see a place for the HIB in today's society? Why or why not?

5. The Soldier Police (SP) in this novel work only for Courtly City. The story implies that other corporate cities may have their own Solider Police forces, which means uniforms and training are not standardized from corporate city to corporate city. Should law enforcement be nationally standardized? Why or why not?

6. Skipper, the elder brother, and Jack, the younger brother argue about ruling Courtly City. Tradition dictates that the older brother should have control, but in this case, Jack, the younger, was given ownership. How many types of leadership can you name? What do you think about bloodline and tradition appointing leaders instead of leaders being elected by a vote of the people?

≥●≤ Q: Why would you think the citizens of Courtly City believe the "ACA" (Anti Corporate Activity) is synonymous with terrorism?

A: In 2030, government is so small, it basically doesn't exist. The "establishment" is comprised of small kingdoms run by corporations. Why do you think Courtly City and other nearby cities have regressed into mediaeval kingdoms with alliances and enemies?

≥ ●≤ ≤ Q: Percy Snatcher has trouble recognizing faces. What do you know about this condition? Are there other conditions you are aware of which may hamper one or more senses, yet can be overcome so individuals can still work effectively at their jobs?

A: **Prosopagnosia (Pro- so – PAG- no- jha)** (Greek: "prosopon" = "face", "agnosia" = "not knowing"), is also called **face blindness.** People with this condition can recognize other objects but not human faces. Those affected with it, still have their ability to reason, strategize, and make effective decisions.

You have two lobes of your brain. The underside of those lobes is what seems to be impacted by **Prosopagnosia** (*"Pro- so – PAG- no-jha"*) The area is called the "Fusiform Gyrus", which facilitates recognition of faces. Originally, it was assumed that this syndrome resulted from a physical injury. Researchers today surmise it can be something you are born with.

Percy Snatcher, is a character who is trying to live his life as a cunning organizer of the AnCors, while having Prosopagnosia. Percy is determined not to let any diminished sense hinder his goal of being the most powerful at what he views as his job.

≳👤≲ Q: Why are libraries rare in Courtly City in 2030s in the story EDGES?

Sometimes libraries are not available to Courtly City's general public because the information they contain may contradict the message put out by those in power. In some societies, producing physical evidence of verifiable information to prove or disprove a "fact", may contradict the propaganda of these corporation-kingdoms. This could be why Sarah's school Administrators are furious that she would conduct research at Library to disprove the "facts" they are trying to teach the students.

In Courtly City, libraries have faded out of fashion. The people are no longer taught how to work with libraries, how to check on a fact, or research a topic. Instead, that society

4

encourages indifference to facts. Amusing, fun-filled entertainments are preferred.

⸲ 👤 ⸲ Q: How do you think this lone library, managed by librarian Mrs. Libris, has survived?

How is a Library defined in our society today?

(1) Public libraries allow books to be available to the general public.

(2) Public libraries are supported by taxes.

(3) Public libraries are governed by a board (such as the American Library Association) with a focus on serving the public.

(4) Nobody is ever forced to use the services provided by libraries. This means that visiting them is voluntary – not compulsory.

(5) Libraries are free (unless your book is overdue). Frequently, they offer other services to the public such as "meet the local author" events, book sales, magazines, and other electronic formats to read or research, archived old original documents, and more...

Benjamin Franklin and a group of his friends pooled their money and bought books to share with others, forming the very first public library in what was to become the United States on July 1, 1731.

Before the American Revolution in 1776, the founding fathers, such as Ben Franklin, understood that to gain freedom to run our own country without a king, the people had to be educated.

This meant the public needed access to facts. Thus, the concept of a library was viewed as fundamental to satisfy the public's thirst for truth and knowledge. By making these new Americans to be a bright and educated people, it was hoped such citizens would be too smart to be fooled into electing a devious and harmful leader.

The common person would need facts to gain understanding about what was happening in the world around them. The elite had the money and resources to honestly provide those facts to the public. Some of them did so via a "library" during one of the most uncertain times in U.S. history.

Q:Do you think in Courtly City, in the 2030's, the leaders want citizens to be well-educated? Why or why not?

🗣 Q: Describe the character of leaders who feel the only way they can keep control over the population is by also keeping the citizens ignorant of the facts? Which leaders in the news seem to promote factual transparent information to their people? Which try to hide the facts with propaganda?

The following is an open discussion which may require knowledge of current events.

🗣 Q: In Courtly City EDGES, how would Bjorn Esterday's investigative reporting help or hurt the dissemination of objective truth?

🗣 Q: Who is responsible for providing public services, such as libraries, to the people? Is it the responsibility of a citizen-elected government? Or is it the responsibility of self-appointed wealthy citizens to provide public services, such as libraries, to the people?

An example of one wealthy person who created libraries is Andrew Carnegie (think Carnegie Hall). He was a self-taught man. Raised in poverty, he died in wealth. Carnegie's pet project was building libraries between 1882 - 1929, as long as the city agreed to staff and fund these libraries.

.

Carnegie donated over $60 million dollars to an effort he said would "bring books and information to all people". Now, this was right before the Great Depression.

In total, Andrew Carnegie built 2,509 Carnegie libraries. He had 1,689 of them constructed in the United States. That means that by 1930 about half of all libraries in the USA were built by Andrew Carnegie.

💬 Q: List examples of modern day wealthy people who feel obliged to spend money on educating the general population or by providing some sort of helpful public service.
This answer will require knowledge of current events.

💬 Q: Do you think a worker's union is a good or bad idea? Why were unions formed in the United States of America?

💬 Q: In the story EDGES, teachers are required to provide only Administrator approved instruction to students, even if the teacher objects because the information is false. Do you believe public schools are obliged to teach verifiable facts? Why or why not?

🕴 Q: Should there be an organized group which requires schools and Administrations to teach students verifiable facts? Should there be consequences if the truth is not taught?

🕴 Q: Do you think, if an employee is pressured to tell lies, the employee should refuse, or should the employee just follow instructions and continue to spread the lies the boss requires? What are the consequences for either choice?

🕴 Q:How might unions be prevented from becoming corrupt?...

🕴 Consider establishing a set of "checks and balances". First, analyze a system which is corrupted and determine how it got that way. Next, discuss how such corruption could have been prevented. Document the steps needed to have a repeatable process to ensure the goals of a union are serving the people it was intended to defend.

🕴 Q: On the train, the cars are divided by social classes. The train station is where all the classes mingle, but once on the train, they have been separated again. What are you thoughts on this process?

🕴 Q: Train station crowds may reveal that the wealthy tend to either ignore the poor or show disdain for them as if the poor were an unpleasant inconvenience. What is your reaction to this social phenomenon? What do you think should be done about it and why? What does having status in society mean to you?

Some concepts to consider:

1. In 1825, trains carried loads (Coal, cattle, etc). Locomotives could travel for 25 miles at the rate of 8 MPH. This was considered fast. Railroads first built in the United States carried goods from Quincy, Massachusetts to Boston in 1827. In August 1829 the first passenger railroad was built by the Delaware and Hudson Canal Company. Passengers were regularly carried starting in 1833.

2. In the book EDGES, the Courtly City train stations are the most secure structures in the city. These trains allow citizens of all classes to reliably travel to their various destinations. In that world, because of the surprise attacks of the AnCors, the SP, or Soldier Police, halt all wheeled vehicles so that they may have more mobility to track down the AnCors. The AnCors, themselves, use "wheeled vehicles". The Soldier Police want the

roads clear in case they need to chase down AnCors.

🗣 ⧏ Q:Which jobs, do you think, make a person "invisible"? Why?

🗣 ⧏ Q: Do you think that if there exists only poor people and rich people, but no middle class, that the poor will be expected to serve the wealthy in silence? Will this cause the rich to get used to ignoring the poor, almost as if they are not people? Do you think there is a need to treat the poor with disrespect? Why or why not?

🗣 ⧏ Q: Do you think if you work hard, and create something great, you should get rewarded with money and increased social status? What do you think about living in a feudal society where it is expected that you follow the occupation of your parents? Which is better for society overall? Why?

How would you describe the society in which you are currently living? Is it an environment where you can work hard to gain money and status, or is it an environment where you should only work to get the same job as your parents? Why?

👤⚞ Q: Read the excerpts (below) from the book, EDGES, and decide if each person described reflects what is rewarded in our society today or not? Which personality type will advance in our present day society? Why?

Jack is described: *"Jack was the more athletically disciplined of the two brothers from his competitive fencing, his pony polo matches, and his many years of serious training in hand-to-hand combative arts."*

Skipper is described: *"...would never engage in such exhausting encounters. Rather he devoted his attention to fashion and parties. Skipper is always the foppish figurehead..."*

Is a Skipper personality going to advance more over a Jack personality in modern society?

👤⚞ Q: What is your reaction to Proverbs 21, "The desire of the lazy man kills him for his hands refuse to labor. He covets greedily all day long..."

👤⚞ Q: In the book EDGES, Skipper tells his brother Jack not to worry. Jack feels that to accomplish a goal, he must worry that it gets done. If Jack does not do the work, the work is left undone. Jack does not trust Skipper and will not delegate work to Skipper. Skipper's track record shows Skipper will agree to do something, then will avoid the task. Do you think this clash of personalities is common in modern families and society at large? How would you deal with a coworker who was like Skipper? Do you get offended when you are frustrated about a task, yet told to "calm down" or "don't worry"? Why do you have that reaction?

❦ ⸖ Q: Have you ever worked in teams in which you are the one who works with tenacity, and perseverance, but you are paired with a person who seems to be quite happy to let you do all the work? What happened to interactions in that team? Did you accomplish the goal?

❦ ⸖ Q: Review the EDGES character descriptions. Do you think the ethics of a parent get passed on to the child? Will Jack pass his ethics on to Ace? Will Skipper pass his ethics on to Pip?

❦ ⸖ Q: Queenie seems to be more concerned about her cosmetics than about the conflicts brewing between the children. Do you think all parents must deal with being self-absorbed to the point of ignoring a situation like that of Pip and Ace fighting over a jacket nearby? Do we all focus on ourselves and ignore the emergencies which require our immediate attention? How can we structure our priorities so that we pay attention to what is really important? Are we so concerned about our own interests that we are blind to what happens around us? Are we substituting technical savvy for human interaction? Are we losing the ability to interact productively on a personal level? Is technology distracting us or is it helping us form better relationships? Do you view yourself as caring and compassionate, as Queenie does, yet come off as aloof, shallow and indifferent?

🎙 Q: In Courtly City, the offices of civilian police are intertwined with military soldiers. These SP (Soldier Police) are owned by the corporation-city. Why do you think this is in the interest of Courtly City societal goals?

Points to Consider
1. Traditional police have the power to investigate and arrest.
2. Traditional soldiers have the power to attack and kill, as part of the strategies they are ordered to follow.

14

3. In the book EDGES, both organizations are utilized to ensure safety and security for the citizens who do not have a national military to defend them. They are combined into one function for the safety and security of upper management at Courtly Corporation. Therefore. we find the position of Offense and Defense are combined into one force. In this Courtly City society, each corporation owns the city, is responsible for trade between cities, and is also responsible for the safety of the citizens of that city.

🗣 Q: What are your thoughts regarding the HIB (Holographic Image Badge) in EDGES?

Points to consider:

1. The HIB contains more information about the individual than a standard driver's license. The HIB contains the occupation (which is why Sarah is called "Teacher Paradise", not "Ms Sarah Paradise"), the status of that person in society, if they can travel or not, etc.

2. The SPs are the only ones who address citizens by their occupation instead of a Mr. or Mrs. etc. How do you feel about that? Would that be helpful in a modern society to have the enforcement team know so much about the citizens? Or, you think there is value in

keeping your personal information more private?

♟ ⛉ Q: In EDGES, the Comm seems to be similar to a phone, but the SPs have "communications devices" which allow them to immediately communicate with each other. The train porters have another channel to communicate with other locomotive staff. In the future, that technology almost devolves into a system which limits free access to information and also limits free contact to others. This means that if Sarah does not have a comm, she is not able to communicate with teachers, school personnel, or reporters such as Bjorn. Since teachers and reporters all disseminate information, they are permitted to be in the same contact class. How do you think this would work in modern society to have technology actually prevent you from talking to anybody you want, but only allowing you to speak with those within your class?

♟ ⛉ Q: What are your thoughts about the Earth Farmers: Ruth Lantz, and her husband Noah, and their son Joshua? In such a technical society, is there room for a non-technical sub-culture?

Points to consider:
1. What is your opinion of groups who remove themselves from society such as the

Amish, Shakers, Mennonites, and other "God-revering cultures" who respect the natural resources of the earth? They eschew electronic technology, opting for the purity of "the old ways and traditions".

Open Discussion

🗣 ⸘ Q: Equality amongst classes appears to have vanished from Courtly City. There is the upper class which is to be served by the poor lower class. Not many middle class left.

Do you think that today, after long years of "worshiping celebrities", we have been conditioned to accept the idea that special advantages are acceptable for those in power even if they do not merit such privileges?

Q: In your society, are your leaders elected or are they "born to the throne"? How are these leaders treated? Would you change or keep this system? Why?

🗣 ⸘ Q: In EDGES, the AnCors describe themselves as frustrated workers who wanted a union. Others say they are just out for whoever can pay them the most money to execute a mercenary job? Do you think an ongoing conflict could exhaust the citizen's emotions and resources to the point that the conflict is simply accepted instead of resolved?

If war is accepted as a way of life, is the loss of life also accepted?

During traditional war-times, orphanages are needed to tend to the displaced children. In the Middle Ages, there was also a need to tend to displaced widows. Convents became a haven for displaced women who wanted to focus on education and spiritual nourishment instead of fighting a war. If a village was plundered and attacked, the women lost their homes and could flee to a convent while the men sought shelter in a monastery. Is providing such shelters useful? Why or why not?

In EDGES, the Widows' cloister becomes a destination of refuge because people are losing their loved ones in this on-going war. The corporations do not feel obliged to care for these unproductive commoners, these defenseless widows, so the "people of God" have taken on that responsibility.

Do you think we need more places of refuge today for those displaced by war and territory disputes? Do we need more convents and monasteries or should this situation be handled another way?

1. What do you think about a friend's "addiction" to virtual reality entertainment? How do you think addiction is evidenced? What do you think you should do if somebody needs help?

2. People often need to get another job to supplement their income. What are your thoughts about those who have finished their schooling but need to take on extra jobs to pay the bills? What should a single person be able to afford on one salary? What should a family (two spouses and two children) be able to afford on one income?

3. In EDGES, one character is creating a castle for himself. Is this over compensating for jealousy, or feelings of inferiority?Why?

4. If you had unlimited amounts of money, how would you spend it? Would you help others ? Why? Why not? Draw parallels to ancient methods of rule and how the people usually reacted to those ancient leaders.

5. *Tho I walk in the midst of trouble, God will revive me. You will stretch out your hand against the wrath of my enemies. (Psalm 138:7).* Why do you think a person could resent a stranger just because of the group that stranger represents? Have you ever experienced such resentment against a stranger? Have you been the target of such resentment? What is the best way to handle this? If a physical fight occurs, what is the responsibility of witnesses or onlookers? Why do you think some people would "take a bullet" for a stranger?

🗣 *Discuss the following with somebody who has not yet read the books. Explain the story briefly, then discuss some of these topics. Be prepared for the possibility that the discussion may take on a different direction than you had originally anticipated. Have the books available for reference.*

1. Document the steps needed to acknowledge an addiction, especially an addiction to a thing which is not consumed by the body (such as games, the internet, or virtual reality, or augmented reality). Do you need to remove the source (the game)? For how long? Do you need to see what events drive that person to play

the game to the point of excluding their other obligations? What are some examples?

a) NOTE:In the 1990's video game rehabs started, but today with the increase of interactive virtual reality games, more and more people are using gaming as a way to avoid dealing with their real-life problems

b) In the story EDGES, one character is on this train because a family therapist advised a vacation in the country, away from servants and other distractions- so that the child could better bond with the family. In your opinion, is this an effective approach? Why? Why not?

c) List an activity you participate in which may stop you from interacting productively with others. What are you using to avoid your obligations? Why?

d) Do you think this is an effective philosophy: *Correct your child and your child will give you rest. Yes, your child will give delight to your soul. Proverbs 29:17*

e) How would you feel if you had a close relative who used bribery get their child out of difficult situations and then your parents expect you to always act with integrity and deal with the consequences of your own actions, refusing to help mitigate that difficult situation?

2. What are your thoughts regarding an individual being able to acquire an entire city or state and run it like a monarch, according to their rules?

a) If you are able to buy a city, should that give you, the buyer, the right to run that city according to your own whims? Or should the buyer, you, obey the rules of the nation in which that city is located? Why?

b) If you bought a bankrupt city, where would you first focus its resources? Would you first set up military protection to guard your city? Would you set up trade agreements with the owners of other bankrupt cities? Would you collect tax or pay tax to a larger city or state? Why?

c) In 2013 the following local governments filed for bankruptcy (see 'v'). Look up each one and answer the following questions to see if you can discern a pattern common to all of them.

    i. How many local governments (city, county, state, or other) have filed bankruptcy recently?

    ii. How are these places doing today? How do you think the bankruptcy impacted them?

    iii. How would things be if they never filed for bankruptcy?

    iv. Did they file for bankruptcy because a corrupt scheme stole money from them?

    v. Bankrupt Local Governments

        1. Michigan- City of Detroit

        2. California- City of San Bernardino

        3. California - Town of Mammoth Lakes (later dismissed)

        4. California- City of Stockton

        5. Alabama- Jefferson County

6. Pennsylvania - City of Harrisburg (later dismissed)

7. Rhode Island - City of Central Falls

8. Idaho - Boise County (later dismissed)

3. The AnCors in this story represent a group which started in order to avoid the abusive treatment the workers experienced in corporations. But, the leadership of this organization got corrupted and now commits the same crimes they claim they are against. What characteristics do you see in the AnCor group? Do they destroy what they disagree with instead of trying to understand and resolve? Do they blame others for failures instead of taking on responsibility for their own actions? Do they look to make a profit regardless of the harm it may cause? Do they think that to win, the other needs to lose and there can never be a "win - win" situation? Do you agree with the AnCor characteristics or not? Why or why not?

4. One assumption is that an addiction is something which absorbs your focus and attention to the point that you neglect your

other obligations. Do you have anything in your life which takes up so much of your attention that you neglect your family, school, or work obligations? Why do you think that is? Do you think sometimes people hide in their obsessions because there is an issue or situation they want to avoid? Why or why not?

5. The AnCors seem to loathe the Earth Farmers. In Courtly City, the Earth Farmers are considered a protected minority. They help generate a food supply for the citizens of Courtly City. In exchange, the leadership at Courtly City created roads for the Earth Farmers to ride using horse and carriage. The Courtly City leadership agreed to purchase food produced by the Earth Farmers. The AnCors do not have a protected status and do not offer anything to help the citizens of Courtly City, so they have instead taken on any task which pays them money.

a) Why do you think the Earth Farmers were able to negotiate an agreement, but the AnCors were not?

b) Is it right that an AnCor, such as Percy Snatcher, should feel resentment toward the Earth Farmer?

c) Do you know of a group of people who are so resentful that they would rather see the other party hurt instead of figuring out how they can improve their own lives?

6. Why do you think the SPs have such technically advanced uniforms? If you could design a uniform for a soldier police officer, what features would it have and why?

7. The AnCors have older vehicles which run on gasoline. The SPs drive modern vehicles which run on clean energy. Why do you think the AnCors are stuck with the older technology for vehicles and weapons? Does it have to do with their attitude that they don't want to change? Or does it have to do with their access to new technology?

8. If you could design a city like Courtly City, where the buildings collect solar energy and the vehicles run on clean energy, how would you set up the city?

a) What would you make available to all citizens?

b) How would you allow for bicycles or horse traffic?

c) How would vehicles get maintained and refueled? How would you transport people going to work? How would you transport large goods which may need to leave your corporate city and travel to another city?

d) Would there be roads between cities, or would you need to have vehicles which can travel on any terrain? How would you keep cargo and people safe when travelling from city to city if Soldier Police only protect the city itself?

e) What geographic location would you select for your city and why?

f) How would your citizens get adequate amounts of water supplied?

g) What would be the source of energy?

h) How would workers get paid? What would the money look like and would it have a technical function?

i) What sort of jobs would your citizens have available to them?

j) What product could you export or trade with other corporate cities?

k) What would be your marketing "slogan" to attract tourists to your city?

l) If there was an emergency, what system would you have in place to keep your citizens safe?

m) How would you deal with trash and waste disposal?

n) How would you allow your citizens to communicate with each other and with those outside of the city?

o) How would you educate the children in this corporate city?

p) How would you set up areas of entertainment for the citizens of your corporate city? Would you have outdoor parks? Which outdoor activities would you promote? Which indoor activities would you promote? Would they include museums? Restaurants?

q) How would you punish people who broke the rules? Would you have a jail in your city?

r) Would you have places of worship in your city?

s) Would you have hospitals in your city?

t) What is the mission statement of your city? What do you stand for and what sort of reputation do you want to have among other cities?

u) What would you name your city?

EDGES Book 1-Swift Encounter

Chapters Covered

✓ 1 CHAPTER Year 2030: Sarah, Bus Stop, Library Card, and the ACA (Continuous Ch 01)

✓ 2 CHAPTER Year 2030: Train Station- Bad Kill, Slash (Continuous Ch 02)

✓ 3 CHAPTER Year 2030:Percy Gets Jack's Photo (Continuous Ch 03)

✓ 4 CHAPTER Year 2030: Encounter Between Jack and Skip (Continuous Ch 04)

✓ 5 CHAPTER- Year 2030: Slash Attacks the Conductor (Continuous Ch 05)

✓ 6 CHAPTER Year 2030: Sarah Meets Bjorn During ACA (Continuous Ch 06)

✓ 7 CHAPTER Year 2030: Body In The Luggage Bay (Continuous Ch 07)

✓ 8 CHAPTER Year 2030: Ace, Close That Window (Continuous Ch 08)

✓ 9 CHAPTER Year 2030:Horse Ride to Library (Continuous Ch 09)

✓ 10 CHAPTER Year 2030: Sarah's Book Lesson (Continuous Ch 10)

✓ 11 CHAPTER Year 2030: Slash And The Soldier Police (Continuous Ch 11)

✓ 12 CHAPTER Year 2030: The Metal Case Flies (Continuous Ch 12)

Discussion Topics Book 1 Swift Encounter

1. Let's do some judging of a book by its cover: What is the book's setting or genre as predicted by the cover illustration?

       a) A western

       b) On a farm

       c) A circus

       d) A military enclave

       e) Something else?

2. What might be the relationships, if any, among the illustrated characters on the cover of the book?

   a) *Leader Hint*: (Chapter 1) Discuss what students think the cover tells them.

   b) Does the cover image reconcile with the contents of the book after students read the book?

3. Why should Sarah's library card be described as "antique"?

   a) _Leader Hint_: (Chapter 1) Why does Sarah's attitude toward the library card give the reader insight into the way the Courtly City citizens think about public places of accessible knowledge?

   b) Is Sarah aligned with popular opinion or is she contrary to the public opinion about libraries? Why do you think that?

   c) What did you think about the lesson Sarah gave her students to teach them how to turn pages on a paper book? How would you suggest keeping a skill alive for the next generation? What skills do you think are important to pass on to the next generation and what skills could be forgotten?

4. The citizens of Courtly City seem to reference "Library" instead of "the Library". Why do you think this society does not use the article "the" in front of the noun?

   a) _Leader Hint_: (Chapter 1) If the concept of public accessibility to knowledge is being stamped out by those in charge, perhaps the society does not know how to properly reference this building or the concept of "library". They use the arcane word but may not feel comfortable using it in spoken language.

   b) How do you think speech and language would be impacted if something you are used to having as a public service was denied for so long that very few people ever realized it had actually existed?

5. Do you find Sarah's character to be empathetic? Why? If not, why not?

   a) *Leader Hint*: (Chapter 5) Analyze the character. Compare and contrast Sarah to any other character in the book and discuss the similarities and differences between the characters. What elements make the reader empathize with a character (in fiction or real life)?

   b) Sarah has to take public transportation to work and then gets her plans abruptly interrupted. How have you dealt with interrupted plans?

   c) Was Sarah right or wrong to have asked a stranger, Bjorn, the question which got her a horse back ride to Library?

   d) Should she have just followed the SPs orders to get a refund and let the kids figure it out when Sarah would just not show up at Library?

   e) What are your thoughts about keeping promises or appointments which are inconvenient?

6. Why do you think Sarah Paradise continues to work under the directives of her bosses, the school "Administrators", who appear hostile to her using the public library for research to augment her teaching?

   a) _Leader Hint_ (Chapter 1) Do you think that large organizations control their inhabitants/ employees/ attendees by the way they present information to the public?

   b) Why do you think some groups are concerned about the general public learning true and objective facts?

   c) Do facts matter or not? Does evoking emotion become more important than finding the truth?

7. How would you respond if you learn that your boss ("Administrator") could, and would, reduce your wages to punish you at any time and for any reason?

   a) _Leader Hint_: Discuss what is considered a "right" assigned to all people equally. Should the public have an expectation of "rights" or "fair treatment"?

8. How does Sarah's environment in Courtly City evidence signs of severe neglect?

   a) *Leader Hint*: (Chapter 5, and 6)

   b) Soot filled fog.

   c) Train station once grand, now dilapidated.

   d) Oblivious wealthy avoiding the despised poor.

9. What characterizes the society in which ACA (Anti-Corporation activity) is announced as a dangerous general threat?

   a) *Leader Hint*: (Chapter 6) Discuss parallels and contrasts between Courtly City society and another society which you may have learned about.

   b) What indicates that the SPs of Courtly City force had once been civilian police? What events do you think took place to convert the force to be militarized soldier police?

c) *Leader Hint*: (Chapter 5) "SP" or "Soldier Police". The book does not describe the transition events which converted the Courtly civilian police force into a militarized force, so ask the group what events could have occurred in this society to cause this transition?

d) Could that transition happen to modern day civilian police? How or why? Why not?

10. The book does not explicitly state a consequence, but what do you think might happen if Sarah is found to be in possession of her "antique" library card?

a) *Leader Hint:* (Chapter 10) What does "confiscated" mean in this society?

b) How might Sarah be punished for violating the directives of the society?

c) Does wanting to preserve a library card make Sarah a "criminal"? Why or why not?

11. *Leader Hint*: (Chapter 3) Describe the personalities and immediate goals of "Slash" and "Percy".

12. What problem does Percy Snatcher have which can hamper his activities?

a) *Leader Hint*:(Chapter 4)

b) "Pro-so-pag-no-sia", the inability to recognize faces

13. How do you think a handicap or impairment impacts Percy Snatcher's ability to lead the AnCors?

a) *Leader Hint*: (Chapter 4)

What makes somebody assume leadership for a good cause or a bad cause? If you have a desire to lead, what sorts of choices would you need to make which could put you on a "good" path instead of a "bad" path?

b) What could convert a good leader into a bad leader? Does character have anything to do with such a choice?

c) How might the people you associate with impact your decisions for honorable versus destructive choices?

14.   Why does Bjorn Esterday need to get past the train station barrier?

a) *Leader Hint*: (Chapter 6) Bjorn is a reporter at the Daily Memo and wanted to "talk to the guy in charge". Why does Bjorn believe he can pass the barrier which was set up to keep all other civilians out?

b) Do you feel that certain restrictions should not apply to you, but should apply to others? Why?

15.   Describe Bjorn Esterday.

a) *Leader Hint*: (Chapter 5) What aspects of Bjorn's character make him likable?

b) What do you not like about him?

c) What would you change about Bjorn?

d) Have you ever wanted to change another person? Why?

16.   Bjorn pushed his way through the crowds to ask the SP to get past the barrier so he could get his story, but he was denied. What do you think of Bjorn's reaction?

a) *Leader Hint*: (Chapter 5) Do you think that if he were admitted and got his story, Bjorn would have helped Sarah?

b) Do you think that if Sarah's plans had not been interrupted by the ACA, meaning she does get to board the train, she would still have met Bjorn?

c) Do you think that sometimes circumstances which interrupt your plans may actually force you to take a turn in your path, and that turn may have been better than your original plan? Give an example.

d) What do you think of the concept of thanking God for your interrupted plans, and can you see the new opportunities presented to you because of those changes?

17. Which character in the book do you relate to the most?

a) *Leader Hint*: (Chapter 9) What first impression did you get from that specific character? What aspects of that character could represent your own character? Why?

b) In your own words, describe what you like and dislike about each character:

☐ Sarah Paradise

☐ Bjorn Esterday

☐ Widow Medicina

☐ Jack & Queenie Courtly

☐ Skipper Courtly

☐ Pip Courtly

☐ Slash

☐ Percy Snatcher

☐ Mrs. Libris (librarian)

☐ Train conductor

☐ Ruth & Noah Lantz and their son Joshua

☐ Messenger who gave Sarah the news at Library

18.   If you were in Bjorn's situation, what might you do to deal with that police barrier at the train station?

a) *Leader Hint*: (Chapter 6)) What tools do you use to deal with a situation like being blocked by a barrier?   Bribe? Blame?   Threaten?   Wait   patiently? Socialize to pass the time?   Meet new people who have also been stranded? Go back home and abandon your original travel plans?   Or something else? Why would you react that way?

19. How did Bjorn get to the train station so quickly with all transportation locked down?

   a) *Leader Hint:* (Chapter 6) Bjorn rode the company horse.

   b) Why does the Daily Memo Newspaper have a horse stable in this society?

20. Ruth Lantz chose to NOT get frustrated when Slash kicked over her sewing basket and then barked at Ruth, saying "bad Earthie". Was Ruth's reaction right or wrong? Why?

   a) *Leader Hint*: (Chapter 4) Have you ever faced rudeness by somebody in a hurry? How do you react when they get mad at you when you are just minding your own business?

   b) How did you handle it?

   c) What do you think of Ruth choosing to not get angry and choosing to NOT bark back, instead forcing herself to have patience?

21. Joshua Lantz, Ruth's son, came by to help Ruth clean up the spilled sewing bag. Can you think of a time when you went out of your way to help somebody clean up a mess?

   a) *Leader Hint*: (Chapter 4) How did Slash act when he kicked Ruth's sewing supplies? Do you agree with how Ruth reacted?

   b) Have you offered to help somebody and gotten an unexpected reaction? Why or why not?

22. What is the important question Sarah wants to ask?

   a) *Leader Hint*: (Chapter 5) What would push you to ask a stranger for a favor as Sarah did?

   b) If you were asked a favor by a stranger, how would you react?

   c) Is there a situation in which you would help or not help?

23. How does Queenie Courtly respond when the two adolescents are scuffling as she is awaiting to board her train?

a) *Leader Hint*: (Chapter 4) Why is she absorbed with applying her lipstick in a public place?

b) What does that say about Queenie's concerns and what she values as important?

24. What do you think Queenie Courtly's interaction with the elderly woman tells us about Queenie's character?

a) *Leader Hint*: (Book 2 Chapter 1 discusses the interaction from Book 1 Chapter 8) What actions or words does Widow Medicina say to convey this impression of Queenie's character?

b) What does Queenie think of herself for her action? Is she teaching or boasting?

c) Can you judge a person's character by how other people react to them?

d) What is it about the elderly woman's behavior which conveys that the woman is devoted to Queenie Courtly as a loyal subject or as an ardent fan?

e) How have you expressed your devotion to another person or celebrity?

25. Why does the scene described on pages of Chapter 9 of Book 1 seem familiar?

   a) *Leader Hint*: (Chapters 6 and 9) The scene is depicted on the cover of Book 1.

   b) What question does Sarah ask of Bjorn?

   c) How does Bjorn respond to Sarah's request?

26. Sarah took time out to explain the concept of Library lending books to the general public. What are your thoughts on free public services like libraries?

   a) *Leader Hint*: (Chapter 10) Do you think the things which are second nature to you today could be forgotten by future generations...like how to even turn pages in a book?

27. Why did Bjorn leave so abruptly?

   a) *Leader Hint* (Chapter 9) Do you think Bjorn jumped to a conclusion? Have you assumed somebody rejected an offer you made for a reason you did not intend?

   b) How will you react next time?

c) Bjorn asks Sarah for her contact information. Why does Sarah refuse?

28. Bjorn galloped away when Sarah did not give him her contact information. What do you think Bjorn assumed?

a) *Leader Hint*: (Chapter 9) Have you felt rejected when you asked for something reasonable from somebody, but they refused?

b) Did you think that they did not give you their time, contact, or other attention because they were rejecting you or because they really were not able to give you what you requested?

c) When somebody asks you for a favor, what is your first response?

29. How did the general public of Courtly City view the library?

a) *Leader Hint*: (Chapter 10) The Courtly City public does not use the library, since the government already provides the information the society should consume.

b) What are your thoughts about objective verifiable evidence gathered through research and analysis?

30. Slash and Percy Snatcher seem to be focused on targeting Jack Courtly, the leader of Courtly City. Why do you think Percy and Slash and the AnCors would have taken this assignment?

a) *Leader Hint*: (Chapter 11) What would have motivated them to take this assignment?

b) What could have been done, theoretically, to make them want to turn down the assignment because it was "wrong"?

c) Where do you think the general Courtly City population gets its definition of right and wrong?

31. What is confusing to the children about Sarah's library card?

a) *Leader Hint*: (Chapter 10) The card doesn't "do" anything. What do the children expect from the library card?

b) Do you expect the gadgets around you to provide more from their basic function? Why?

32. What has gone wrong with Slash and Percy during their terrorist AnCor mission?

a) *Leader Hint*: (Chapter 12) Why is Slash not with Percy? What has happened with their mission? What happens when Percy signals Slash?

b) Has there been a time when you made plans and they all fell apart? What did you do? Did you move forward with the "mission"? Or abandon it? Or did you blame others?

33. Slash gets caught by the head porter who says Slash cannot board the upper class train car. Was this right or wrong?

a) *Leader Hint*: (Chapter 4) Do you feel sympathy with the porter? the Courtly family? or Slash? Why?

b) Do you feel you have acted in a manner which told another person that they were not allowed in a certain area, but you were?

c) What was the situation?

34.   How does Percy view Slash? How does Percy move on?

   a) *Leader Hint* (Chapter 12) Slash shows devotion to Percy.   What is Percy's attitude toward Slash? How does Percy show his attitude toward Slash?

   b) Have you witnessed an unbalanced relationship where one party is devoted and the other party shows no empathy?

   c) Was that relationship productive? How might it be improved?

35.   Percy seems to want to keep Slash close, but also seems to want to get a better companion. Why?

   a) *Leader Hint*: (Chapter 12) Once you feel "I can do better" because you feel superior to the other party, do you think you are still "in that relationship"?

   b) Do you think it is just a matter of time before that person feels that you are not committed to that relationship?

   c) Have you been in a relationship where you felt tensions escalate quickly into an unpleasant disagreement? How was this situation resolved?

36.   Why do you think the news paper Bjorn works for, The Daily Memo, has a horse for the reporters?

a) *Leader Hint*:   (Chapter 6) Do you think the society you live in could ever get to the point where transportation becomes unreliable? How might that happen?

b) What modes of transportation would you use if four-wheeled vehicles (like cars) become unavailable to the public.?

c) What infrastructure would need to be in place to support an alternate mode of transportation?

d) How would that impact your daily routine?

37.   How is Andrew Carnegie connected to the development of public libraries?

a) *Leader Hint*: (Chapter 14) Do you think if somebody reaches a certain level of wealth, they should contribute to society by providing a service for the people, like libraries, hospitals, or something else to help the population?

EDGES Book 2-Rousing Attack

Chapters Covered

- ✓ 1 CHAPTER Year 2030: Game Locked Away (Continuous Ch 13)
- ✓ 2 CHAPTER Year 2030: Ace Gets Sassy (Continuous Ch 14)
- ✓ 3 CHAPTER Year 2030: Meet The Lantz family (Continuous Ch 15)
- ✓ 4 CHAPTER Year 2030: Jack Arranges A Nice Dinner (Continuous Ch 16)
- ✓ 5 CHAPTER- Year 2030: Where Is Ace? (Continuous Ch 17)
- ✓ 6 CHAPTER Year 2030: One Exit Blocked (Continuous Ch 18)
- ✓ 7 CHAPTER Year 2030: AnCors On Board (Continuous Ch 19)
- ✓ 8 CHAPTER Year 2030: No Way, Lady (Continuous Ch 20)
- ✓ 9 CHAPTER Year 2030: Find the Woman (Continuous Ch 21)
- ✓ 10 CHAPTER Year 2036: Executive Headquarters (Continuous Ch 22)
- ✓ 11 CHAPTER Year 2036: New Summer Job (Continuous Ch 23)
- ✓ 12 CHAPTER Year 2036: Intern Tour (Continuous Ch 24)
- ✓ 13 CHAPTER Year Year 2036: Castle (Continuous Ch 25)

Discussion Topics Book 2 Rousing Attack

1. Have you ever had anybody tell you to stop doing something? Did you think that was an unnecessary request? Why? Do you think that person wanted you to stop for your benefit or theirs?

   a) _Leader Hint_: (Chapter 4)

   b) What did Ace want Jack to do at court?

   c) Why does Jack forbid Ace from playing with the toy?

2. Describe a time when you anticipated a moment only to have it arrive and then you froze and did not know how to act.

   a) _Leader Hint_: (Chapter 2) Why is Ace "horrified"?

   b) How does Percy react when he first bumps into Jack?

   c) How does Queenie react when she first sees Ruth Lantz?

3. Describe a time when you have planned something and those plans are frustrated, how do you express your frustration? Anger? Calm deep breaths? Do you take the time to understand why the other person acted the way they did? Do you ask yourself if your actions contributed to their reaction?

   a) *Leader Hint*: (Chapter 6) Of what are Jack and Noah unaware? Why?

   b) Why is Percy suddenly angry?

4. What guides your moral compass? On what are you willing to compromise? What is definitely "not for sale"? Can you demonstrate acts of kindness without hoping to get something back?

   a) *Leader Hint*: (Chapter 8) How does Noah help Queenie?

   b) How does Percy plan to collect a ransom?

5. Have you ever felt that you were forced to do a task or take on a job because you were at a disadvantage compared to others you know? Did you feel resentful? Did you feel you were exposed to unpleasant elements that you should not have been exposed to? What is the best way to react?

a) *Leader Hint*: (Chapter 10) Where and when do we see Sarah Paradise again?

b) How would Sarah describe her reaction to her new boss?

6. - What are your thoughts about student apprenticeships in corporations?

   a) *Leader Hint*: (Chapter 10) Is the company looking to employ "slave labor" or to provide a good work experience for students?

   b) Will Sarah return to teaching students at her school, or will she join the company? Why?

7. -What are your thoughts about a corporate boss who is acting inappropriately and expecting you to NOT use your expert skills for which you were hired?

   a) *Leader Hint*: (Chapter 11) What does Sarah need to do by end of summer?

   b) Why is Bjorn not happy with both Sarah's job and his own job at the paper ?

8. - Should communication channels, such as the post office mail, be available to the public or should it be a "club" reserved for a special few who can pay fees to use the services?

   a) *Leader Hint*: (Chapter 12) What does Joshua tell the group about their farm?

   b) Do you agree or disagree with the way some students react to Joshua's comments as they do?

9. What if your boss asked you to NOT use a talent you have because they thought it may reveal something that they did NOT want to be discovered? How would you handle that?

   a) *Leader Hint*: (Chapter 13) Why is Skipper Courtly's long range goal for other corporations in the area upsetting to Pip?

   b) Why does Bjorn arrive at the old mansion Skipper has just purchased?

EDGES Book 3-One Foot Under

Chapters Covered

✓   1 CHAPTER Year 2030: Execution (Continuous Ch 26)

✓   2 CHAPTER Year2030: One Week Before the Train Leaves (Continuous Ch 27)

✓   3 CHAPTER Year 2036: Sarah Needs to Bring Something (Continuous Ch 28)

✓   4 CHAPTER Year 2030: Camp AnCor (Continuous Ch 29)

✓   5 CHAPTER-   Year 2030: Mass Grave (Continuous Ch 30)

✓   6 CHAPTER 2030: Welcome Back, Slash (Continuous Ch 31)

✓   7 CHAPTER Year 2036: A Dancing Date (Continuous Ch 32)

Discussion Topics Book 3 One Foot Under

1. How do you prepare for an unexpected catastrophe?

   a) *Leader Hint*: (Chapter 1) What makes Queenie start to cry? Who captures her? Why is she dragged down into the ditch?

   b) What are the AnCors doing as the train pulls away?

2. How do you avoid getting fooled by people you must work with, but do not trust?

   a) *Leader Hint*: (Chapter 2) Why does Jack refuse to sign the Mayfounder agreement with Skipper?

   b) What was Skipper's motivation for starting the Mayfounder foundation?

3. Does power and wealth eliminate the need for creativity?

   a) *Leader Hint*: (Chapter 3) Who gives awards to Skipper's son Pip? Why does Skipper tell Pip he does not need ideas?

   b) What does Bjorn want Sarah to do?

4. How do you evaluate the integrity of an organization with which you must engage?

   a) *Leader Hint*: (Chapter 4) What does Jack believe the Courtly Corporation will do for him?

   b) What message does Percy get from Skipper ?

5. What if a decision you make impacts many more individuals than you originally anticipated? How would you deal with the "casualties"?

   a) *Leader Hint*: (Chapter 5) How do you guide somebody who has been removed from society for a serious period of time, either from injury or from another matter?

   b) How do they become acquainted with a changed reality.?

   c) If you were one of the three who was on their way to feed hungry people, but had your trip interrupted by a stranger in need, how would you react?

6. Do you think status symbols elevate you in the eyes of others? How far would you go to acquire these status symbols?

   a) *Leader Hint*: (Chapter 6) Percy felt accomplished the moment he stole Jack Courtly's clothing and put the clothes on. Why do you think Percy took the clothes for himself instead of sharing with his AnCor men?

   b) How does Percy plan to make money on Jack?

   c) What are three procedures the Soldier police uniforms can undergo?

7. If you believe a public institution is supposed to protect you, but then find out that it will not help and may, in fact, harm you, how do you respond?

   a) *Leader Hint* (Chapter 6) What does Jack do to escape?

   b) What do the Courtly SPs do to Jack?

8. How do you measure a friendship? Do you need to keep in touch constantly or can you still be good friends with somebody you have not seen in a long time? How would

you react if they did not want to share details of why they were absent?

a) *Leader Hint*: (Chapter 7) Where do Bjorn and Sarah go when they meet again?

b) What do Bjorn and Sarah discuss?

c) How long had it been since they first met?

9. Suppose you stumbled upon information which was a serious threat to public safety, and was contrary to what the public assumed to be true. Suppose that information pointed to a culprit which was not who the public thought it was. Now, what- if any- is your obligation as a citizen to share that information either with a justice organization or with the public directly?

a) *Leader Hint*: (Chapter 7) What information does Sarah take and pass to Bjorn?

b) What does Skipper do to his corporation when he is told Jack was no longer alive?

10. Slash bursts back into camp, hoping to be greeted as a hero, but instead is greeted with suspicion by Percy Snatcher. Why?

a) *Leader Hint*: (Chapter 6) Would you trust Slash if he told you the SPs do not know your secret location?

b) What would you do if you overheard this interchange between the AnCors?

EDGES Book 4-Earthshake

Chapters Covered

Discussion Topics Book 4 Earthshake

1. What do you think of Bjorn Esterday's assignment to interview Skipper about his remodeling? What would you do if you were Bjorn? What would you do if you were Skipper?

   a) *Leader Hint* (Chapter 1) Why does Skipper insist on calling the basement the dungeon?

   b) How do the workers protect themselves from a law suit?

2. An old factory was converted into a prison for men. Do you think the construction of a factory or plan can be converted to a prison? What are the similarities between a factory and a prison? What construction would need to take place to convert it to a prison?

   a) *Leader Hint* (Chapter 2) How do those at the Widows' Cloister get supplies and repairs

   b) Why does the Eldress question Queenie?

3. Have you ever searched for somebody you have not seen in a while? When you found them, did you expect recognition and did not get it? How did you react and how did the other party respond?

   a) *Leader Hint* (Chapter 2) What does Eldress say that frightens Queenie?

   b) Who rushes into the cloister to get food?

4. Jack overheard a conversation between two others who were plotting an escape. Should Jack have joined in and pledged allegiance to the AnCors? What do you think of what he decided to do? What consequences are there to either choice: Pledging allegiance to the AnCors vs. what Jack chose to do?

   a) *Leader Hint* (Chapter 3) Why does Queenie react as she does when Jack meets her?

   b) Do you agree with what does Queenie does next?

5. -Does Jack deserve to be in prison? Does prison keep Jack safe from his brother Skipper? Does it keep him safe from Percy Snatcher? What would you do if you were Jack? Stay or flee? Why?

a) _Leader Hint:_ (Chapter 4) After seeing Queenie, what does Jack suspect?

b) What do you think the other prisoner wondered when Jack offered to throw out the trash for him?

6. At what point would you allow an injustice to continue? When would you "walk away"? Or does an injustice have to be righted regardless of the personal cost?

   a) _Leader Hint_ : (Chapter 5) What signals everyone that their entire building is in danger?
   b) How does Guard Gene help Jack? Why does he help Jack?

7. Later, Sarah and Bjorn are looking through old newspapers and such for research. How would you conduct research into a topic if all on-line options were not available to you? How would you verify it was "true"? Does being "true" matter? Which is more important: Knowing the true steps which led to an event, or knowing the consistent message put out by the ruling party?

   a) _Leader Hint_ (Chapter 5) Why does the Eldress agree to take them all to the monastery?

b) In her haste, what does Queenie forget?

c) Why does this matter?

d) Have you ever left something behind which resulted in unexpected consequences.

8. How would you react if you discover a place you thought was safe and filled with helpful people is now deserted?

a) *Leader Hint*: (Chapter 6) Does Jack make wise choices as he takes items with him?

b) What does Jack do when he hears people approach? Why?

c) Jack finds something. What does this discovery tell him?

9. Should the wild obsessions of someone close to you be ignored, such as the dungeon and the violin, or should medical help be called?

a) *Leader Hint*: (Chapter 7) Why is Skipper's Castle construction work being furiously rushed ?

b) What is Pip desperately worried about?

10. Sarah had to take a summer job to supplement her teaching salary. What do you think about that practice? Should a salary be enough to allow for some time off during the year?

   a) *Leader Hint* (Chapter 8) What do you think about the way Pip, who is now her boss, is treating Sarah?

   b) Is it right or wrong or unimportant? Why?

   c) What do you think Pip will ask Sarah about the file? Why?

11. What are your thoughts about redaction (blacking out words in a document) of portions of a legal document ?

   a) *Leader Hint* (Chapter 9) What can Sarah do to get the information which was redacted, or should she not be accessing that information? Why?

   b) Where and why does Bjorn join Sarah?

12. How do you deal with somebody in power who thinks they deserve even more power and wealth than they already have, and are willing to disregard integrity to achieve it?

   a) *Leader Hint* (Chapter 10) Why does Skipper want Bjorn to see the castle dungeon

   b) What does Skipper boast about and demand publicity for

EDGES Book 5-Broken String

Chapters Covered

Discussion Topics Book 5 Broken String

1. How would you handle a situation where a person who has more status, power, or wealth than you, believes something you know is false? How would you balance sharing the truth, with tact and courtesy, and a measure of understanding that you may not be able to change their mind?

    a) *Leader Hint* (Chapter 1) What does Bjorn see as he enters the dungeon with Skipper?

    b) What does Skipper believe the ghost will do for him?

2. How do you deal with tasks you feel are boring, ill suited, or otherwise disagreeable? How would you decide to either finish the task or abandon the task and then justify that abandonment to those who expect you to complete the work?

    a) *Leader Hint* (Chapter 2) Why does Bjorn want to stop working on his Skipper article?

    b) What worries Sarah?

3. How far would you go to self-teach yourself a new skill? If you agree to complete a task that you think you can easily accomplish, but then find out that job exceeds your skill set, what would you do?

a) *Leader Hint* (Chapter 3) Why does Sara climb up onto the stone shelf in the dungeon?

b) Why does Sarah suddenly stop working on the cables?

4. List examples of ways you can influence others around you. Why do you think those techniques work or don't work? Would you recognize it if somebody else tried these techniques on you?

a) *Leader Hint* (Chapter 3) What Medieval social technique is Skipper trying to use?

b) What motivates Skipper to adopt such an old technique?

5. How do you evaluate the temptation to short-cut your way to a seemingly more powerful position? How do you discern who you would be obligated to if you took that short-cut?

a) *Leader Hint* (Chapter 3) Why did Skipper send Bjorn away?

b) What does Skipper believe will happen to him?

6. What are ways you can show gratitude to those around you? How do you evaluate what is meaningful to each recipient of your appreciation?

a) *Leader Hint* (Chapter 6) What does Bjorn plan to do to show his appreciation for Sarah?

b) Why is Bjorn given a toy?

7. What do you do each day to ensure you have a consistent reputation for reliability? How would you want others to react if your pattern of reliability was interrupted?

a) *Leader Hint* (Chapter 7) What makes Bjorn suddenly realize trouble is ahead?

b) Why does he feel urgency to address this? What would be the consequences if Bjorn did not act with urgency?

8. If you feel a matter is urgent, how do you convince others they must also take the matter seriously?

   a) *Leader Hint*   (Chapter 8) Who meets Bjorn back at the castle?

   b) What does Bjorn look for on the lake? Why?

9. How would you react if somebody presents you with urgent concerns and asks for your immediate help at an inconvenient time?

   a) *Leader Hint*   (Chapter 9) What overwhelms Bjorn and the foreman?

   b) What happens when Bjorn acts on his instincts?

10.   If all of your "safe" locations have been violated, what can you do to regain your feeling of safety?

   a) *Leader Hint*   (Chapter 10) Where is Sarah? What circumstances put her there? Could she have avoided it?

   b) What causes Sarah to suddenly be alert and frightened?

EDGES Book 6-Key Witness

Chapters Covered

Discussion Topics Book 6 Key Witness

11.   What is the appropriate response to somebody who looks down on others whom he considers to be inferior? If another views you as inferior when you know you are not, how would you react to their insults? Would you discuss this issue with others or would you choose to keep it to yourself and remain silent? Why?

a) *Leader Hint* (Chapter 2) What makes Skipper so upset in the crowded music shop?

b) Why does the clerk's reply make Skipper storm out?

12.   When do you play it safe and when do you take a risk when you discover that the upper management of your organization is corrupt?

a) *Leader Hint* (Chapter 1) What is Bjorn trying to explain to his editor Sammy?

b) Why does Sammy want to reject Bjorn's information?

13.　　What are your thoughts on automation and robotics? How can it help or hurt people? Describe how technology can actually create new jobs?

　　a) *Leader Hint*　(Chapter 3) What leads Bjorn through the Courtly Corporation campus?

　　b) What surprises Bjorn when he arrives at Skipper's office?

14.　　What are your thoughts regarding management's role in the level of worker satisfaction? How should workers react with a leader who has improved working conditions, is now being pushed out by another who only wants the glory of that leadership position and will cause working conditions to decline?

　　a) *Leader Hint* (Chapter 4) Why is Skipper angry when he sees the Board of Directors?

　　b) What do they want Skipper to do? Why?

15. If you go out of your way to help somebody and the recipient does not acknowledge your good efforts and even treats you with disdain, what is the best way to react?

a) *Leader Hint* (Chapter 5) Why is Bjorn annoyed? Which people does he recognize?

b) What does Pip bring to the microphone?

16. Why are people influenced by the enthusiasm of a crowd? Why do people prefer procrastination and distraction instead of just sticking with a task to completion?

a) *Leader Hint* (Chapter 6) Why does the tour group hurry back to the party?

b) What two items does Bjorn discover?

17. How do you define the difference between "meetings by fate" versus "chance coincidental meetings"?

a) *Leader Hint* (Chapter 7) Why are Sarah and Bjorn together? What do they learn?

b) What impels Bjorn to leave?

18. How do you mentally prepare yourself to let go of something you really value but must leave?

   a) *Leader Hint* (Chapter 8) Why do Queenie and Eldress decide to quietly go away?

   b) What does Queenie regret?

   c) What has Queenie learned about priorities?

19. How do you evaluate what could be your next home?

   a) *Leader Hint* (Chapter 9) What do Queenie, Eldress, and Elder James find?

   b) What do Eldress and Elder James discuss urgently?

20. How do you divide the labor so that everybody has equal amounts of work and you all collaborate to build a new home?

   a) *Leader Hint* (Chapter 10) What does Queenie's sign announce?

   b) What is the goal everyone else is trying to achieve?

21.   When you feel you have nothing, why would you risk taking on a fight to free another? Would you confront your enemy in order to save somebody else in need?

a) *Leader Hint* (Chapter 11) What did Jack think and do when he saw Percy Snatcher?

b) Why have the children been captured?

22.   How can you act with integrity and nobility even when life circumstances appear dismal? How might your acts of valor, kindness, and gallantry done years ago reap positive results in the future?

a) *Leader Hint* (Chapter 12) What is Jack reminded of as the children express gratitude?

b) The grateful villagers give food to Jack. What happens to it?

c) Who finds Jack asleep on the ground?

EDGES Book 7-Who is She?

Chapters Covered

Discussion Topics Book 7 Who Is She?

1. - If you have a procedure you must follow, when do you break protocol to do something especially good?

   a) *Leader Hint*   (Chapter 1) Where does Guard Gene take Jack?

   b) Why did Guard Gene use his own money/credits?

2. How do you recover when you jump to an incorrect conclusion about somebody else's motives?

   a) *Leader Hint* (Chapter 2) How does Elder James interact with Jack?

   b) How does Elder James respond when Jack abruptly asks a question?

3. Can you evaluate all the "bad" things that have happened in your life? Can you see a pattern of these incidents as they may have put you on a path you may not have ordinarily taken? Can you see that these experiences may have honed skills or allowed you to meet somebody you would not have otherwise met?

a) _Leader Hint_ (Chapter 3) Why is Elder James suddenly called away?

b) Is Jack's presence going to surprise somebody?

4. What would you do if you recognized somebody you have not seen for many years and that person does not recognize you?

a) _Leader Hint_ (Chapter 4)What does Sarah prepare as she waits for Bjorn?

b) What happens when she opens the door expecting to see Bjorn?

5. How do you keep calm when confronted by a surprisingly stressful event?

a) _Leader Hint_ (Chapter 5) Why is Sarah now a target?

b) How does Sarah react to an unexpected visitor?

6. Under what circumstances would you feel prompted to investigate somebody's identity?

a) _Leader Hint_ (Chapter 6) Why did Sarah's visitor hide?

b) What does Sarah learn about the identity of the SP?

7. How do you judge somebody's credibility when they give you information?

   a) *Leader Hint* (Chapter 7) What does Sarah's dinner guest reveal to Bjorn?

   b) How does Bjorn realize his "wheeled vehicle" and passenger are in danger?

8. How do you evaluate your need for self-protection over following standard protocol?

   a) *Leader Hint* (Chapter 8) What do the chase vehicles try to do to Bjorn's wheeled vehicle?

   b) Why does Bjorn refuse to file a report about what happened?

9. If you had access to valuable information, what would you do to protect your source, and also share the information with the person you can trust, but carefully hide the information from untrustworthy or dangerous people?

   a) *Leader Hint* (Chapter 9) Why do Sarah and Bjorn search for their now missing dinner guest?

   b) Who comes back through the window?

83

10.   Do you hold cultural biases? Do you think that if a person is from a particular cultural demographic, that they should react to a situation in accordance to their culture and maybe not to yours? For example, would farmers understand how to build a robot?

a) _Leader Hint_   (Chapter 10) How did Alexandra originally get the device someone else is after?

b) How does Bjorn find out who attacked him?

c) Who is Alexandra?

EDGES Book 8-Vanish

Chapters Covered

- ✓ 1 CHAPTER Year 2036: I Looked The Other Way (Continuous Ch 75)
- ✓ 2 CHAPTER Year 2036: Celery (Continuous Ch 76)
- ✓ 3 CHAPTER Year 2036: Inside the Violin (Continuous Ch 77)
- ✓ 4 CHAPTER Year 2036: Changing Pictures (Continuous Ch 78)
- ✓ 5 CHAPTER- Year 2036: Faded And Disappeared (Continuous Ch 79)
- ✓ 6 CHAPTER Year 2036: Bjorn Calls the Foreman (Continuous Ch 80)
- ✓ 7 CHAPTER Year 2036: Coffee with An SP (Continuous Ch 81)
- ✓ 8 CHAPTER Year 2036: Who Is Harry? (Continuous Ch 82)
- ✓ 9 CHAPTER Year 2036: A Glass of Bubbly (Continuous Ch 83)
- ✓ 10 CHAPTER Year 2036: Caged (Continuous Ch 84)

Discussion Topics Book 8 Vanish

1. What do you think of traditions like growing celery to prep for a wedding?

2. Why do you (or don't you) think community should get involved in ceremonies like births, deaths, and weddings?

3. If you were told to not use a skill you have because that skill may embarrass a person in power, what would you do?

   a) *Leader Hint* (Chapter 1) What is Sammy Scribe demanding from Bjorn?

   b) What does Bjorn want Sammy to do, and why?

4. If somebody you care about is heading into a dangerous situation, what are your thoughts about following that person into the situation to offer help or protection?

   a) *Leader Hint* (Chapter 2) Why is Joshua waiting outside Sarah's apartment building?

   b) Why did Joshua get permission to work at Courtly Corporation?

5. If your job description has clearly defined limits, why would you go beyond those limits to right a wrong? Or is it better to drop the issue and pretend it never happened? What is the consequence of either choice?

   a) *Leader Hint* (Chapter 3) Why does Sarah go into the music store?

   b) What does Sarah ask at the Soldier Police station?

6. How would you react if you felt you were delivering useful information to an authority figure, but in response, they treat you as a nuisance or worse, they accuse you of malfeasance?

   a) *Leader Hint* (Chapter 4) What happens to Sarah at the SP station?

   b) What does Sarah want to find out at the Daily Memo?

7. Should private citizens be concerned about how corporations dispose of their waste? What is the appropriate action a private citizen should take?

a) *Leader Hint* (Chapter 5) What does Bjorn learn from following the Mayfounder truck?

b) What shows up behind Bjorn?

c) With what tools does Bjorn improvise his actions ?

8. Should important information be delivered in person or can such information have the same impact if delivered over other forms of communication?

a) *Leader Hint* (Chapter 6) What must Bjorn do as he is trying to call on his communication device?

b) During his call, what does Bjorn find out?

9. Are uniforms, which identify individuals as trained professionals, essential to inform the public about the validity of the skills these individuals can genuinely render? What should be the consequences of people who wear the uniform but do not possess the needed skills of that profession?

a) *Leader Hint* (Chapter 7) How does Harry Liteman react when he sees the SP?

b) What information does the SP learn from Bjorn's questions?

c) Why did Bjorn head into that particular hydration station?

10. What do you think about business executives supporting technology and automation without a plan to re-educate those displaced by that technology so they can get new productive jobs?

a) *Leader Hint* (Chapter 8) Where and why does everyone gather together?

b) What does the drone car do?

11. Have you ever succumbed to flattery, only to discover that the person heaping praise on you really meant you harm? How did you handle that? How do you discern the difference between a genuine compliment and mere flattery?

a) *Leader Hint* (Chapter 9) What happens to Bjorn in the large warehouse?

b) What does Pip find out after he drinks the champagne?

12.   Describe a time when you felt trapped. Did you develop or do you already possess any skills iwhich can get you out of your predicament?

a) _Leader Hint_   (Chapter 10) Where does Bjorn find himself ?

b) How does Bjorn escape?

c) Who does Bjorn discover, and what does Bjorn do? Why does he do this?

EDGES Book 9-Chase or Die

Chapters Covered

Discussion Topics Book 9 Chase or Die

1. Can hot air balloon transportation, as seen in Courtly City, happen in today's modern world?

2. Have you ever been so driven to find the answer to something that you did not let anything stop you from getting to your goal? Why were you so motivated?

> a) *Leader Hint* (Chapter 1) Where does Bjorn find his quarry?
>
> b) How is Bjorn able to recognize his quarry?
>
> c) Is Bjorn able to capture the suspect in time?

3. In your opinion, what is the value of festivals and other organized community activities?

> a) *Leader Hint* (Chapter 1) What events occur in your area which attract large crowds?
>
> b) Why did this Courtly City festival originally start? What reason did the festival serve the people? Is the original reason for this event still valid as Bjorn enters the fair grounds?

4. Describe a time when you yearned for something and then, when you got it, the reality of your wish either shocked or disappointed you?

  a) *Leader Hint* (Chapter 1) What is Bjorn's motivation for his intense search?

  b) What shocks Bjorn when he suddenly realizes the true identity of his quarry?

5. Do you think the decisions of one individual make a difference to the general good? Do you feel that your choices impact others?

  a) *Leader Hint* (Chapter 1) What might happen to the people Bjorn knows if Bjorn fails to catch his quarry?

  b) If Bjorn fails in his mission for justice, how will the citizens of Courtly City be impacted?

6. How do you evaluate your options before making a decision? Do you consider how you feel? Do you think about the impacts your choice has on others? Do you objectively consider the facts?

a) *Leader Hint* (Chapter 1) Do you think Bjorn is wise or reckless taking the risks he does? Why?

b) If you were in Bjorn's place, would you continue to confront the danger Bjorn faces? How would you do it?

7. Sometimes people boast about making grand gestures to impress others, but what are your thoughts on paying attention to acting in a considerate, empathetic manner to the people you see regularly? .

a) *Leader Hint* (Chapter 1) How would you handle the situation if your pursuit of justice resulted in endangering innocent bystanders?

b) What would make you stop your pursuit? What if you realize your opponent is better equipped than you?

8. If you have been forgiven for an offense, would you extend that same courtesy to others who have offended you?

a) *Leader Hint* (Chapter 1), Do you think money or power insulates a person from consequences of breaking the law?

b) If powerful wealthy people break the law, should their punishment be different from an average person violating the same law? Why?

9. Do you consider yourself somebody others can count on even if they are unable to pay you back for the favor?

a) *Leader Hint* (Chapter 2) Did Sammy hurt or help Bjorn's situation?

b) Do you think Sammy Scribe is somebody Bjorn Esterday can count on or not?

c) How do the SP (Soldier Police) get involved?

10. Describe a situation where you might be able to help somebody realize their honorable, but unspoken, heartfelt dream?

a) *Leader Hint* (Chapter 3) Describe the gift-giving mixups.

b) Describe everyone's reaction when Detective Gene enters with the new visitors.

11. Have you evaluated your own behavior to be sure you are NOT being hypocritical; that you do NOT have two sets of standards, one for you and another set for everyone else.

    a) *Leader Hint* (Chapter 4) How do the AnCors justify their criminal behavior?

    b) If a group says they believe in freedom, but support their fight for freedom by abusing and enslaving others, would you believe what they say or would you make your judgement based on what they do?

12. Why do you think some people ignore a plea for help from a stranger instead of rendering aid?

    a) *Leader Hint* (Chapter 4)How would you get the people of Courtly City to care, act, and fight on the side of justice when powerful people engage in criminality ?

    b) How would you convince a group of people that its worth it to them to regularly engage in the maintenance of true justice?

EDGES Terminology & Vocabulary

In the world of Courtly Corp, Bjorn Esterday and Sarah Paradise and the others who live there often use special words. This section shares the definition of those words.

1. **ACA   Anti-Corporate Activity** - The ACA is sounded publicly by the SPs when their sensors pick up the presence of the AnCors. When an ACA alert is in progress, no wheeled vehicles are permitted on the pathways. This is to allow the SPs on horseback to chase the offender.   During an ACA, citizens are permitted to use trains, horses, or any other mode of transportation without wheels. Since the AnCors use older gasoline-powered cars and trucks, the SPs know that if those vehicles are on the road, then the drivers are probably AnCors operating those vehicles.   This allows SPs to make their pursuit of AnCors more effective.

2. **Acquiesced** - Agreed with reluctantly.

3. **Adrenalin** - A hormone made by the adrenal glands

4. **AfterShake**- Movement of the earth which follows an earthquake.

5. **Allegiance** - Loyalty to a person, or cause, or government.

6. **AnCor / Anti-Corporatists** - This group has many locations, but the one located in Courtly City at the time of this writing is headed by Percy Snatcher, who relies on his subordinate, Slash.

The AnCors started as a protest to the increasing abusive power of corporations against its workers, but bit by bit, the members were cut off from resources by the very corporations they tried to fight. As a result, those who are a member of the AnCors at the time of this writing live "off the grid" of the corporate kingdom. They use older technologies of the past, abandoned by the citizens of the corporate city.

They also have learned to survive by selling their mercenary talents to the highest bidder, which, hypocritically, embodies the very spirit of "anything for a profit" which they claim they are trying to combat in formal corporations.

The AnCors refuse to acknowledge their own hypocrisy by claiming to fight for freedom while, at the same time, they engage in kidnapping and then selling defenseless villagers into slavery, as well as killing for hire.

7. **Antiseptic** - Relating to substances that prevent the growth of disease causing microorganisms. Disinfectant.

8. **Apologetic**(apologize)-Regretfully acknowledging an offense.

9. **Appreciative**- Showing or feeling gratitude.

10. **Berate**-Scold or criticize someone angrily.

11. **Biurnal** - (See diurnal) This is a term created for this story

12. **Break room** - A place to briefly go to get refreshment .

13. **Brilliant** - For light or color:bright, shining. For people: very talented, genius, creative.

14. **Canvas** - Close woven cloth of flax, cotton or hemp on which a picture is painted. Also used to make sails for a boat.

15. **Clandestine** - Kept secret or done secretively.

16. **Cloister**- A convent or protected, secluded, quiet place.

17. **Concussion** - A brain injury caused by a blow to the head or violent shaking of head.

18. **Debris** - Trash, rubble, wreckage.

19. **Deadmail** - Courtly City slang term for redmail. This term was created for this story.

20. **Dehydration** - A significant loss of body fluid that impairs normal body function.

21. **Dismal** - Dreary, depressing, dim, gloomy.

22. **Distress** - Extreme anxiety, sorrow, pain

23. **Diurnal** - (referencing biurnal) Takes place during the day. Happens every day.

24. **Earthie** - This is a disrespectful term used to refer to a member of the Earth Farmer Community.

25. **Earth Farmers** - The Earth Farmers are a fictional group of people who eschew the technology of the modern world in Courtly City and instead quietly and peacefully live and hone farming and other hand-craft skills, including but not limited to quilting. They are considered a peaceful religious community.

26. **Earthshake** - An archaic translation would be "earthquake". This is a term referring to the shaking of the ground and, at times, to the point of opening a fissure. This term was created for this story.

27. **Effervescent** - Fizzy, carbonated, sparkling, frothy, bubbly.

28. **Ethical** - Relating to moral principles. The branch of knowledge dealing with morality.

29. **Goodies** - Sweet foods to eat, or objects that are fun to collect.

30. **HIB** - Holographic Identification Badge. This is the identification device carried by Courtly City citizens. The SPs will fit the HIB into a slot on their forearm sleeve, which will provide full details of the citizen on the SP's visor display. This is why SP's address the citizens by their profession instead of Mr. or Mrs. For example, "Reporter Esterday" and "Teacher Paradise". This society defines each person by their occupation.

31. **Inheritance** - A birthright, heritage, legacy, the practice of passing on property

32. **Injustice** - A wrong, an infraction of the law, against the truth or facts.

33. **Intravenous** - Given into a vein.

34. ***ipsa scientia potestas est*** This is a Latin term used by Mrs. Libris, the Librarian. The phrase was penned by Francis Bacon in 1597. Some translate it to mean "Knowledge itself is power" which Mrs. Libris applies by encouraging the children from Miss Paradise's class to become powerful, honest, honorable citizens armed with factual truth."

35. **Jailbirds** - Slang reference to a person who was, or is, in prison (or jail).

36. **Justice** - Fairness, right, equity, legality.

37. **Lilliputian** - A very small person or thing. Referred to by Jonathan Swift in the book Gulliver's Travels.

38. **Molecules** - A group of atoms bound together in the smallest unit of a chemical compound to take part in a chemical reaction.

39. **Mystical** - Relating to supernatural, occult mysterious experiences.

40. **Optimistic** - Hopeful and confident about the future.

41. **Patience** - Being able to accept delay, trouble, or suffering without getting upset.

42. **Potential** -Having the ability to develop into something successful in the future.

43. **Prosopagnosia** (Pro- so – PAG- no-jha) (Greek: "prosopon" = "face", "agnosia" = "not knowing"), is also called face blindness. People with this condition can recognize other objects but not human faces. Those affected with it, still have their ability to reason, strategize, and make effective decisions. You have two lobes of your brain. The underside of those lobes is what seems to be impacted by Prosopagnosia ("Pro- so – PAG- no-jha") The area is called the "Fusiform Gyrus", which facilitates recognition of faces. Originally, it was assumed that this syndrome resulted from a physical injury. Researchers today surmise it can be something you are born with.

44. **Quarry** - Usually a large, deep pit from which various minerals can be extracted.

45. **Raucous** - Making a disturbing, harsh, loud noise.

46. **Redact** (redacting, redaction)- Cover up or censor part of a text to hide the words from view.

47. **Redmail** (see deadmail) This is a term for redacted mail received electronically. RED = Redacted Electronic Document. Deadmail is a nickname given by those in Courtly City to redacted electronic mail because at times the document is so redacted that there is no

readable meaningful content. This term was created for this story.

48. **SP** - Soldier Police - Military personnel which are the enforcement body assigned to protect each corporate kingdom. Each city provides uniforms and procedures for their own SPs. The ones who work for Courtly Corporation have special technically advanced uniforms. This term was created for this story.

49. **Statuary**- Three dimensional representations of people, animals etc modeled in clay, bronze, marble, and other minerals.

50. **Statue** - A carved or cast figure of a person or animal that is usually life-sized.

51. **Surmise** - To guess something is true even without evidence to confirm it.

52. **Surmised** - Past tense of "surmise". Guessed something was true without having confirmed it.

53. **Unethical** (unethically) - Not morally correct. Deceitful, unfair, dishonest.

54. **Vital signs** - The essential body functions including heart rate, breathing rate, blood pressure, temperature, oxygen saturation, capillary refill time.

55. **Warehouse** - A large, plain building for storing goods. A warehouse is used by businesses, manufacturers, wholesalers, etc.

⁞ End ଓ

ABOUT Wynter Sommers

Wynter Sommers is the pseudonym for an American writing team, which harnesses multiple skills in technology, research, and education. Formally trained with a PhD in Education, Wynter Sommers blends academic classroom experience, with corporate sophistication, and a passion for developing more effective student insights.

Wynter Sommers has taught classrooms of enthusiastic children. She has a heart to inspire creativity and develop critical thinking skills, all to encourage students to make wise choices in life. She emphasizes honing one's skills in developing self-reliance and collaborative team work. Despite any environmental barriers beyond an individual's control, Wynter Sommers wishes to impart the message that genuine hope, love, and peace can help us overcome obstacles and develop friendships. Wynter Sommers hopes you enjoy the other *Bjorn Esterday* stories in this series.

ISBNs and Bar Codes

✧ **Edges Book Bundle Set**
(9 Books + Conversation Station Book= 10 Books)
- 978-1-7184-0012-2
- 1-7184-0012-8

✧ Edges Book **1-Swift Encounter**
- 978-1-7184-0002-3
- 1-7184-0002-0

✧ Edges Book **2-Rousing Attack**
- 978-1-7184-0003-0
- 1-7184-0003-9

✧ Edges Book **3-One Foot Under**
- 978-1-7184-0004-7
- 1-7184-0004-7

✧ Edges Book **4-Earthshake**
- 978-1-7184-0005-4
- 1-7184-0005-5

✧ Edges Book **5-Broken String**
- 978-1-7184-0006-1
- 1-7184-0006-3

✧ Edges Book **6-Key Witness**
- 978-1-7184-0007-8
- 1-7184-0007-1

✧ Edges Book **7-Who Is She?**
- 978-1-7184-0008-5
- 1-7184-0008-X

✧ Edges Book **8-Vanish**
- 978-1-7184-0009-2
- 1-7184-0009-8

✧ Edges Book **9-Chase or Die**
- 978-1-7184-0010-8
- 1-7184-0010-1

✧ Edges Book 10-**Conversation Station**
- 978-1-7184-0011-5
- 1-7184-0011-X

www.ingramcontent.com/pod-product-compliance
Lightning Source LLC
Chambersburg PA
CBHW051840020726
47502CB00005B/1884